SECRET of the OLD BARN

Written by Adrian Robert
Illustrated by Penny Carter

Troll Associates

Library of Congress Cataloging in Publication Data

Robert, Adrian.
Secret of the old barn.

Summary: The secretive new neighbors arouse curiosity with their unusual life style.
1. Children's stories, American. [1. Neighborhood—Fiction] I. Carter, Penny, ill. II. Title.
PZ7.R5385Sg 1985 [E] 84-8743
ISBN 0-8167-0412-0 (lib. bdg.)
ISBN 0-8167-0413-9 (pbk.)

Printed in the United States of America.

10 9 8 7 6 5 4 3 2 1

SECRET of the OLD BARN

Scott and Jenny and I were looking out my bedroom window at the White Elephant. That's what everybody calls the house next door. Jenny and Scott Sawyer live on one side of us. The White Elephant is on the other.

"I hope the new people are nice," Jenny said.

"I hope they have some kids our age," I said.

"I hope they fix the place up," said Scott. "That house has gotten spooky standing empty!"

The White Elephant looks like it must be haunted. It has three floors and a tower and lots of porches. It has a great big barn and lots of land in back. In the front yard a sign said HOUSE FOR SALE.

HOUSE
FOR
SALE

That Saturday afternoon Mr. Carson tacked up another sign: SOLD.

"Let's go ask who bought it," I said. We ran downstairs.

Mr. Carson grinned when he saw us coming. He knew what we were going to ask.

"All I know is their name's Cadwallader," he said. "No, I don't know if they have any children. But Mr. Cadwallader looked pretty old."

Mr. Carson's pretty old himself. If *he* thought Mr. Cadwallader was old, things didn't sound hopeful. Jenny sighed. I kicked a stone.

"Don't give up too soon, Mark," Mr. Carson said. "The Cadwalladers asked if it was all right to keep animals in the barn. They asked for a house that had a lot of rooms."

"Oh, boy!" Scott shouted, and turned a cartwheel.

"They *also* asked for a quiet neighborhood." Mr. Carson frowned at us, pretending to be stern. "I said this place should suit them fine. So don't you three make me out to be a storyteller."

"We can be quiet as mice when we have to," I told him. I just hoped we wouldn't have to.

After that day a lot of things happened. Workers came and fixed the White Elephant's roof. They mowed the grass on the front lawn. They left the grass in the back meadow high.

Then the men started working on the barn. They cranked the whole place up with a big machine. They built a new floor under it and put up new siding. This was getting interesting.

"I think we should go see if we can help," I said. Scott agreed. We climbed over the fence. When we were halfway across the meadow, one of the men saw us.

"You kids get out of here!" he shouted. "It's dangerous! You don't belong here!"

Scott and I decided we didn't want to help with their old barn after all.

Next some young men started fixing the shutters and the broken windows. They swarmed over the White Elephant like monkeys. One of the men had a black mustache and tattoos. On one arm he had a heart that said MOTHER. On the other arm he had a pirate flag!

Jenny's eyes grew large. "You don't suppose the Cadwalladers are pirates, do you?" she whispered.

"Of course not!" Scott said. I didn't feel too sure about that.

That night I told Mom and Dad what we'd seen. "Don't let your imagination run away with you," Dad told me. He says that to me a lot.

Mom just laughed. "I'm sure the Cadwalladers will be nice neighbors. Look how they're fixing up the White Elephant!"

Before long, the White Elephant did look pretty nice. The walls of the house sparkled with fresh white paint. The shutters glistened blue. There were red geraniums on the porch railings. But the house still stood empty. Scott and Jenny and I spent lots of time hanging around watching. We wanted to see the Cadwalladers move in.

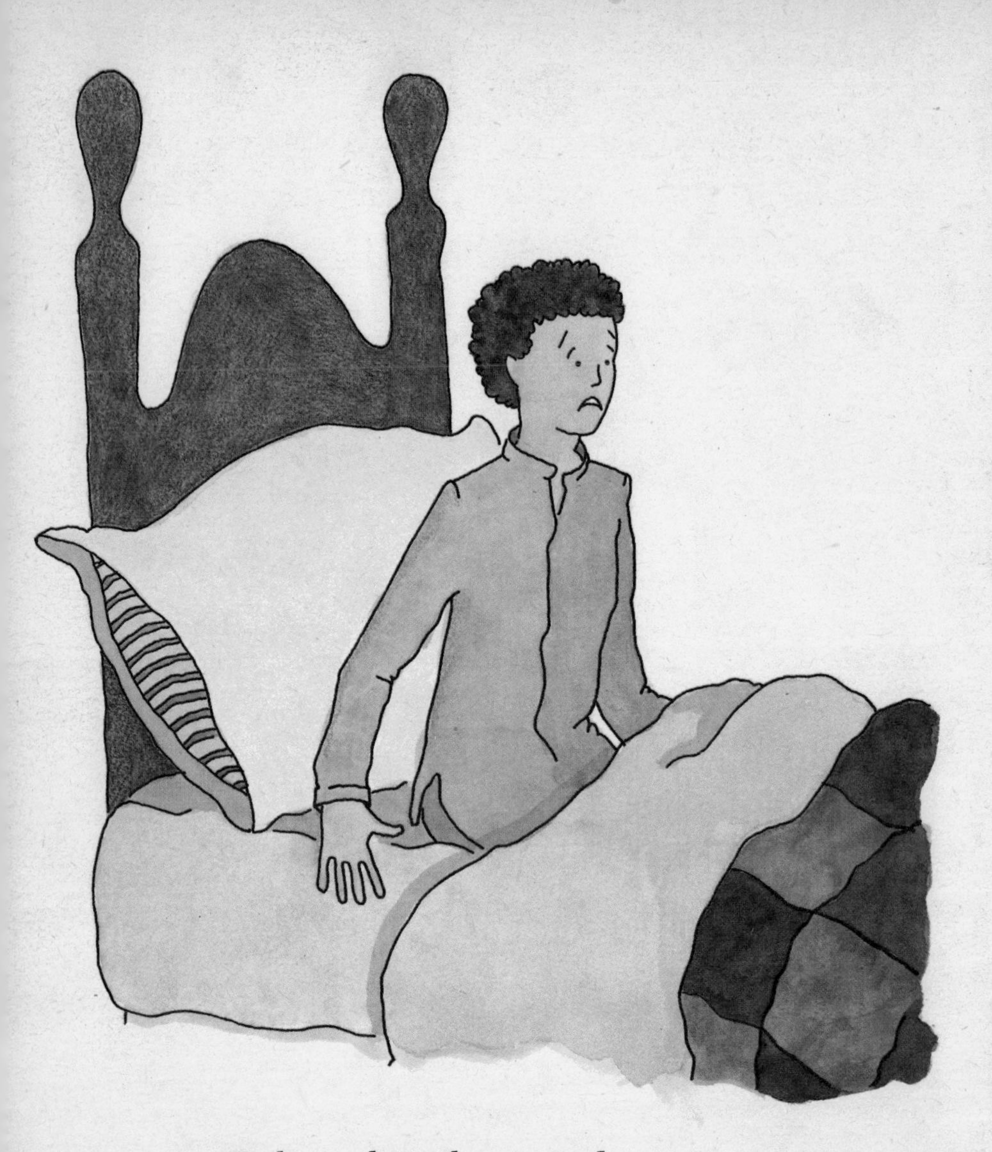

Only nothing happened.

Then late one night, I heard a noise. I sat straight up in bed. Then I heard it again. *EEEEEEEKKK*. Wheels were creaking slowly.

I ran to the window. Outside, it was completely dark. But there were lights on in the White Elephant. People were carrying furniture into the house. The Cadwalladers were moving in—in the middle of the night!

I pulled off my pajamas. I pulled on my jeans and shoes. Then I ran into dad, standing in my doorway.

"Oh, no you don't," Dad said firmly. "You can meet the Cadwalladers in the morning."

But in the morning all the shutters were closed. There wasn't a soul around. There was just a huge van backed up against the barn's double doors.

Over the weekend a tall wire fence went up around the back fields. "That's not a nice way to treat neighbors," said Scott.

"A lot of things are funny," I said. I told them how Mom had gone to visit and found nobody home. I told them how she tried to telephone the new neighbors. But the operator told her there was no phone listed for Cadwalladers.

"You know what else?" I said. "I hear cars come in late at night. I see lights go on. But look at the house now." The shutters were closed tight.

"It sure is weird," Scott said. "It's like they've got day and night mixed up."

"Maybe they *are* pirates," Jenny said.

We decided it would be a good idea to keep a watch on the White Elephant. Scott and I hung around the fence a lot that week. Once we saw the tattooed man. Otherwise we didn't see anybody. With his dad's field glasses, Scott tried to read the writing on the van. He looked hard. Then he passed the glasses to me. I tried too.

"There's too much dirt," I said. "It's as if the mud was there on purpose."

Suddenly we heard a sound coming from the barn. *E-E-E-E-E!* It was creepy.

"Did you hear that?" Scott whispered. "It sounds like somebody shouting through a trumpet! Only I never heard a *person's* voice sound that way!"

I told my folks. You can guess what they told me: "Tell your imagination to stop worrying, son."

I told it. It didn't do much good.

Guess what happened the next day. I looked out the back window and saw a *horse* in the meadow. It was a brown horse with a silver harness and pink plumes. A girl was riding it bareback. Round and round they went.

I ran outside. Scott and Jenny were at the fence already.

"Hi!" Jenny called.

The girl and the horse galloped over.

"I'm Jenny," Jenny said. "I live in the green house. This is my brother Scott. And that's Mark. He lives right next to you."

The girl smiled. "I'm Angie. And this is Wildfire." She patted the horse's neck, and Wildfire whinnied.

"You want to come play?" Jenny asked. I knew she was hoping Angie would invite us to play with her and Wildfire.

"I can't," Angie said. "I have to work."

"Was that Wildfire we heard making strange noises yesterday?" I asked.

Angie looked scared. "I don't know what you're talking about," she said. She dug her heels into Wildfire and galloped away.

"Weird!" Scott said.

After that I didn't know what to think. Maybe I *was* imagining things. But I was worried.

A few days later, I was sitting alone on the porch. Mom was at the store. Wildfire wasn't in the meadow. I could hear her whinnying somewhere. Suddenly, I heard that sound again. *E-E-E-E-E!* It was coming from the barn. And then I heard "Help! Help! Save me!"

Quickly I ran next door to the White Elephant. The shutters were closed. I looked up. Somebody was walking along the top of the roof!

I wondered what to do. Then I heard *"Help!"* again. It sounded like Angie. Maybe robbers were breaking in! Maybe they were holding Angie captive!

I knew I couldn't wait. I ran up the front steps and rang the doorbell. I banged hard on the door.

The door swung open!

I was in a big room filled with furniture. Suddenly Angie came through a doorway. She wasn't hurt. But when she saw me, she looked scared.

"What are you doing here?" she asked.

"I heard you call for help," I whispered. "Are you O.K.?"

I could hear someone coming. An old woman appeared. She had a bright green parrot on her shoulder. The parrot walked down her arm and yelled, *"Help! Help!"*

I asked Angie, "Why didn't you tell me it was a parrot?"

"I'll explain, Angie," the woman said. She smiled at me. "We're the Great Cadwalladers. Angie's my granddaughter. She's not allowed to tell people about us. Some neighbors don't like our animals. They tease them. They don't let us alone. Some neighbors are nosy."

I turned red. Mrs. Cadwallader smiled again. “You’re different,” she said. “You were worried about Angie. You wanted to help her. You’re a good neighbor.”

"Animals?" I asked. "You mean there are more besides Wildfire?"

"Why don't you take this young man to the barn and show him?" Mrs. Cadwallader said to Angie.

The parrot flew to Angie's shoulder and came with us. Angie scratched the parrot's head. "This is Webster. He's in our act, too."

"Act?" I said. This was not making any sense.

Angie grinned. She opened the barn door.

Inside the barn was a circus ring! Wildfire was trotting round it. She wore the silver harness and pink plumes. The tattooed man had on a silver suit. "That's my Uncle Ernie," Angie said. "He's a high-wire artist. So's my Dad. He's practicing on the roof right now. My Mom and my Grandpop are trapeze fliers. We're The Great Cadwallader's Imperial Circus. I'm the

bareback rider," she added proudly. "And that's Samantha."

Angie walked across the barn and stood next to a baby elephant! Samantha was the one who had made the trumpeting sound!

I took one look and started to laugh. "You know what this house is called?" I said. "The White Elephant! But we never thought there'd be a real elephant here!"

Mom and Dad met the Cadwalladers that night. They kept telling my folks what a good neighbor I was. Scott and Jenny and I got passes to see the circus. And Angie even lets us ride Wildfire sometimes.

I wonder if the Cadwalladers could use a bareback elephant rider.